RABBITBOX

ALSO BY WAYNE HOLLOWAY-SMITH

Alarum
Love Minus Love
Lobsters

RABBIT BOX
WAYNE HOLLOWAY-SMITH

**SCRIBNER
EDITIONS**

London · New York · Amsterdam/Antwerp · Sydney/Melbourne · Toronto · New Delhi

First published in Great Britain by Scribner Editions,
an imprint of Simon & Schuster UK Ltd, 2026
Copyright © Wayne Holloway-Smith, 2026

SCRIBNER and design are registered trademarks of The Gale Group, Inc.,
used under licence by Simon & Schuster Inc.

The right of Wayne Holloway-Smith to be identified as author of this work has
been asserted in accordance with the Copyright, Designs and Patents Act, 1988.

1 3 5 7 9 10 8 6 4 2

Simon & Schuster UK Ltd, 1st Floor, 222 Gray's Inn Road London WC1X 8HB

For more than 100 years, Simon & Schuster has championed authors and
the stories they create. By respecting the copyright of an author's intellectual
property, you enable Simon & Schuster and the author to continue publishing
exceptional books for years to come. We thank you for supporting the author's
copyright by purchasing an authorized edition of this book.

No amount of this book may be reproduced or stored in any format, nor may it
be uploaded to any website, database, language-learning model, or other repository, retrieval, or artificial intelligence system without express permission. All
rights reserved. Inquiries may be directed to Simon & Schuster, 222 Gray's Inn
Road, London WC1X 8HB or RightsMailbox@simonandschuster.co.uk

Simon & Schuster Australia, Sydney
Simon & Schuster India, New Delhi

www.simonandschuster.co.uk
www.simonandschuster.com.au
www.simonandschuster.co.in

The authorised representative in the EEA is Simon & Schuster Netherlands BV,
Herculesplein 96, 3584 AA Utrecht, Netherlands. info@simonandschuster.nl

Simon & Schuster strongly believes in freedom of expression and stands against
censorship in all its forms. For more information, visit BooksBelong.com.

A CIP catalogue record for this book is available from the British Library

Trade Paperback ISBN: 978 1 3985 5242 5
EBOOK ISBN: 978 1 3985 5243 2
AUDIO ISBN: 978 1 3985 5244 9

*This book is a work of fiction. Names, characters, places and incidents are either a
product of the author's imagination or are used fictitiously. Any resemblance to actual
people living or dead, events or locales is entirely coincidental.*

Typeset by Marsha Swan

Printed and Bound in the UK using 100% Renewable Electricity at
CPI Group (UK) Ltd

—

in all of her broken-
ness she told him
close your eyes
and see it waiting
like a heartbeat
you can take off your
shoes and float in
lie back shush now
she sang like a home
that doesn't hurt
as do all good breaking
mothers a song
that had known him
all its life

—

PERHAPS ALL LANGUAGE BEGINS HERE

                                      24 Coalbrook Street
and the mind caught between its layers of wallpaper
or the mind pulled like carpet across the floor-
boards creaked and cranking grey, immaculate

horrible carpet stretched over a home
grown badly and filled up with thinking –

    he sat THERE, it says, broiling in his bitter dad-
    chair and the mother, she sat THERE, the mind says,
    without daring a look back over her shoulder,
    the TV on the washing out the whole house
    holding its breath –

                        and it's here perhaps the rabbit
was made and each time made again
in the moments before
all the shattering what-comes-next

24 Coalbrook Street
and the smaller bedroom
is all rabbit boy-rabbit
rubbed over the smell of floor, and starched-rabbit
the ceiling rabbit the duvet, cabinet and toys cocked
the magazines in quarter-
open drawers, rabbit on the lamp switch
thumbprint of rabbit on the wardrobe door

                              open it

  you are allowed
  deep in the clothing stacks to look
  a tiny place
  for minutes years perhaps
  in which he
  uncomfy-sat or
  out the open window pleaded
  into a town
  biting the night-time rotten
  singing:

king of nervous laughter
touched in the wits
a small body hidden
in the wardrobe or else
caught too young
in the guttural clinch
of a home's full wind:
a man whose temper
is bigger than god hurts
if you broke your fingers
against the hope
for something better than this
born into the terrible
hosanna of language
then you know
my name –

worried little creature
shaken in his collarbones   rabbit   see him
back there tiptoeing an all-drunk and angry home
cement home and cigarettes, shovel
and litter home with the hard luck
it taught itself spilled

                              into brick and plywood
                    into every corner and sideboard
              in all the terraced places of the here, now

see him

fistfuls of carpet in the smallest space

cramped under the two-seat sofa

screwed up tight invisible

eyes shut and secret-breathing

the living room's big threat

heated so hard

you can almost hear it crack

the leather cushions

set to sting a backside hot

if there was a backside here

there's not

> the silence knows there's something
>
> on the other side
>
> of this – the ashtray
>
> is piling up its cigarette butts
>
> and he's collecting an emptiness
>
> that hurts for the thing that hurt it:

so enter and keep entering, man-shadow
boots off, soused and wholly home from work
dad-shadow looming its choral might
over the shut curtains, the cabinet
door's hard ringing, the picture frames
stay out the way
while it finds its seat, fist slamming
a thick glass down, full and thirsty
temper like a brass band, sleeping
warming up, eyeing your mother, flinch
her own language is quiet-backing away –
careful, careful – to the kitchen

careful, careful – one slip, rabbit one bump

and suddenly the whole house is awake

and hymnal – a shadow's man-lunge

and *hosanna* the wallpaper is trumpeting

his hand, orchestral, his voice – *hosanna*

the pots some pans a shoe kicked

and the doorframe booms animate

something in him like a fist to the back

always hard blue veins

under dark blue jeans

a mother always

mute over the sink

at the edge of everything

no kind word but the place is ringing

A QUESTION

how many-a-home enunciates its offspring this way:
its song holding a child by the throat
and wrong-deep in its full volume
and how many-an-offspring grows tough
gone off on the carpet, hands over its ears
in the depth of the wardrobe or out
the window and under the streetlights
at the edge of everything, *please*

A HISTORY

SHE

sees him first at a barn dance – as they are called
in this point in history
his muscular shoulder to the barn door she wants
she thinks she wants to be close to touch it
with her right palm – and look, now she is
telling her friend over the music
she is fifteen and something like water
filling the bell of her stomach right up to her throat
and he is just a bit older, there in his oily jeans
his T-shirt white and clung to his chest
the leather of his jacket
and one of those love ballads is slow-playing
is perhaps complicit in what she is feeling
when he looks back at her
for maybe the whole length of that song
and half the next – his eyes and teeth, his cheeks
cleaned shaved in the manner of older boys'
or young men's faces, he doesn't falter
doesn't sip his drink doesn't at any point turn
to speak to his brothers or check

on his motorbike outside the door
such is his confidence he doesn't look away
though she might have expected it –
if he had, or she had moved
to the other side of the hall or moved schools
days ago   as was supposed to happen
or if she'd stayed that night to help her mum
who'd broken three bones in her right foot
maybe her mum would   maybe love would ———
it rained at that moment so heavy
it felt like the world was ended
or begun in a new way

⋆

there exists no photo no evidence
beside her stomach full that night
his eyes and close-shaven cheeks that
muscular not too muscular back she
touched she did actually touch the
rain pouring down like a love song
saccharine on her skin her hair down

to her scalp, no evidence no words for
this feeling she has only her fringe –
a mess of hairspray and water in her
shoes, she is wandering slow drawing
out each long moment she is somewhere outside herself, above, a little
behind, in front now and watching
her own body drifting home much
later than she supposed the night so
beautiful with its ordinary sky

★

there exists no photo but there are
things she kept each time they met
– a ticket stub from the picturehouse, a beer mat folded into her
pocket, the cigarette he gave her once,
a packet of salted crisps and the
secret in her stomach so it could
always be this way and she could also
keep his handsome mouth could

keep the way he wore his jeans, the boyish toughness and the hand he combed his hair back with she'd lock it all up each day and hold it and they could keep being she thought young together and innocent in the back of his brother's car

SHE

felt like the world was ended or begun in a new way
she had *made her bed*   her mum whose three bones
had healed by now couldn't look at her –
what does it mean for a child
or very young woman
to have brought shame back to her home
how one sister sat at the kitchen table
picking from a half loaf of bread
scraped a crust in a near-empty jar of honey or jam
how one sister sat spiteful at the foot
of the carpeted stairs with a smirk on her heart
how does an incredibly young woman or child
carry that shame or weigh it
resolve to take that weight inside herself
keep hidden its growing until it kicks out
and there's no way to conceal it any longer
her mum whose three bones by now had healed or
maybe her dad in his anger couldn't look at her
she had she was told *made her bed* and either way
she had it was said *to lie in it*

SHE

had to lie in it – and did first behind the shops
when he pushed her   with both hands away
and in that moment she knew everything
about desire, that body she fell upon and again
now with pleading – for all of this was
she came to understand her fault alone, her shame
grown busy and sticking right out in the daylight
the bell of her belly

she had to lie in it – and did as she took a knitting
needle to herself and then a hot bath and vodka
in her friend's cast-iron tub and she was sorry
that it might work and sorry that it didn't
so sorry she arrived the rain rifling down
to stand in his yard with its scrap metal, its tall weeds
and she wept until his own mum, or maybe dad
caught sight out the window at the bed she had made
and made him lie in it with her

★

there exists no photo of the chip shop
– the battered sausage heavy-salted
the cod soused in vinegar outside
the seaside registry office with no
family member there to witness or
hold her   the red bench they sat
on two young sudden adults alone
and trying not to contemplate the
bed they had to lie in   there was
no friend or brother free from work
that day, it was ok – she wanted to
believe it, a home of their own fresh
with carpets they could learn to
love a TV set and sofa and a kitchen
with its utensils – it would be ok
the chips the chips were beautiful

★

to begin with
there was the iodine smell
there was the shapeless white and patterned gown
the particular type of alone she felt
the kindness of the nurse's hand
there was the bed she'd made, her husband
smoked somewhere then smoked again
there was nothing readable on that male doctor's face
there was the needle
for more than a moment there was nothing at all
the shift inside her, like weather
the wrench the wrench
emptying herself was a type of dying she hung
upon the wall   there was the screaming
they pulled from deep within her
outside it rained and she somehow travelled
round the night – its dark and glittering map
and when drenched and hardly with a voice
she was returned to herself
a pink thing dropped down through the ceiling
and landed on her lap

A QUESTION

how far can a mother's comfort travel
when a home's choral syntax grows
big calamity in the living room
furious clambering its walls, round the ceiling, drinks
cabinet clanged open and rattling hubris, how far –
when she's frozen in the bruised kitchen –
can a mother's kindness reach   into the mind
of a child steeped in his hiding place,
red-cheeked and sad and scruffed at the neck,
and whomsoever could deliver it, that kindness,
as most language dies in its falling:
pennies dropped from some great height
perpetual copper into the nowhere fast forever

whomsoever can deliver it, that kindness,
and when did you begin –
simple as wanting – to appear
to him in his rabbithood, O Alma
a tiny girl with bows in her hair
crunched up with him
beneath the leather sofa
or holding him behind the wardrobe door
– that fragile little thing
shaken in his collarbones
with a shadow-dad's thick racket
always crowding in – one clenched hand
one boot one pot a banging pan at a time

O scrappy Alma scrunched beneath the sofa
and Alma with those bony shoulders
behind the wardrobe door
the tangled kindness of your hair
and nose that's smudged with dirt
the little freckles on your cheeks
with all the noise outside making it hurt
O plucky Alma's plucky hand upon his knee –

                    how far can a mother's comfort travel
                          echoing in that present tense
                                    were you worried
                                        into being
                                     his buck teeth
                                    your name, Alma
                                    thrown against
                                         the skin
                                       of his shut
                                            lips

                simple as wanting –

the mother before the home fell
truly into all its bad
the mind recalls
the tender arms she had
when he'd be ready for sleep
she'd lull him to the magic of a riverbed –

the story of a young rabbit
and his small imagined friend
how they did sneak
from underneath
a castigating home
out past its garden
with the lonely washing on the line
along a daunted alley
its pavement cracks
and upturned trolley
then found their way
across the town
through its tunnels' dank
and over a field
to sit there
and be small
on the river's safe
and grassy bank

and he would lie then on the pillow
and think the relief of trees the heartbeat of water
he would think the comfort of the other children there
the mother said that the young pair watched
them slow-moving and illuminate
and he would lie and think
the young girl untying her shoes
think the rabbit taking off his socks
and be away
beneath the sky
despite what else
the mind recalls
everywhere here right then, thank you
was ok

                                        a bad home's chorus
                                            a shadow-dad
                            – one hand one pot one shoe one pan –

and from all this distance
the mind recalls
how much it mattered
each time inside the wardrobe
Alma
back there
rinsing off the mother's bedtime tale
young voice keeping the two of them
from all that's shuddering-terrible
down the stairs
the slow insoluble sad-aching

and the mind recalls –
stretched like carpet across the floor,
staring from the Artex ceiling or
folded into the layered paper on the walls –
the mother one time locked herself unable
behind the door of the downstairs toilet
to elude the rage that thumped against it
and the mind recalls the dinner cold upon the table

        how all of her voice then was a picture
     of a couple of kids dreaming of that river, Alma
          new hope with its trousers rolled
            bathing them in that story
       and away from things they hadn't left yet:
       a mum's sore hands, shame, the fat banging
             of a father's rancour
              despoiling a kitchen,
               the giving way
                of the downstairs
                  toilet door
                    where –
                     please

hold my breathing while I recall again

my own lungs

from

the dead

sat up skinned

alive and

lifted as they are from inside the wardrobe

I AM

I AM

king of nervous laughter
pinned by fear
against a magnolia wall
a silhouette
lit up like a chip shop
if your worry was told
it was the wrong way round
and the yelling made sense
but didn't feel right
if your ears were pricked
against the interior night
and the no of childhood
was limed with anger –
its teeth stained by cigarettes
if you grew up under
the punishment of shadows
understood only by their wet hand
on your neck
then you know
my name

A HISTORY

SHE

has these hopeful premonitions that go smudgy around the edges – first a house and through one window she thinks herself inside, she makes out the boy – she's sure of it now, mirroring his handsome father – the light of early evening tilting

through the kitchen there's a drop-leaf dinner table, the boy's hair yes is combed and he's playing with his food – watches his dad, the homemade chips he swirls around in ketchup and does it just the same, when his dad coughs he too musters up a sputter, there's a sip of beer in his plastic see-through cup, and she knows she'd die for him when he practises shaking the pages of his comic straight licks his thumb

SHE

has these hopeful premonitions a young family smudgy round the edges – they are making faces in the bathroom mirror, she thinks her face is only slightly older, her husband now has sideburns and all their eyebrows frowning-funny-faking scary, toothpaste foaming up their mouths the husband barking like a wild dog and the boy – he howls and howls so pleased with himself on that plastic step he needs to reach up to the bedtime ritual above the sink's enamel

SHE

came to know how quick a bed is coloured different
when there's nowhere else to return to
nowhere else to put your head down
when the other person wants to do things
you don't want to do, or hasn't washed
and when the other person's breath is wracked
with alcohol   she came to know
her many faults   his hand raised up
his cheek unshaved   and never never answer back
the living room shifted when he got home
from work, this one time
he didn't like the food
she taught herself to cook and so he ———
and when all she needed
was to call her mum
she cleaned the house instead

THE MOTHER'S BEDTIME STORY
(A FRAGMENT)

there was once a boy with a twitching pink nose
and a fluffy tail and kneecaps and there was a home
which held him in its fist – its squeeze tight –
and shouted its yelling in his face

    and its language made

childhood hidden in a wardrobe

    and its language made

wild thumping anger and bumps
and clatter as loud as cowbells

    and its language made

in the boy with buck teeth and elbows a grief so great
he must have conjured her in his shaking: a girl his age
and somehow older came it seemed from somewhere
inside his crying

he felt for sure the whole of her history grow with him
beneath the home's conceited ceiling

and it came to pass weeks and bellowing unkind hands
and it came to pass a looming shadow
with its erratic rage
and it came to pass one night they packed a knapsack
or didn't a lunchbox or satchel and snuck out or didn't
they left or tried wriggling free of the fist and set out in
search of a magic river

A QUESTION

how long has that water been there –
still, moving somewhere in his cotton dreaming,
probably not long, probably a very long time
on the edge of a blinking eye
when there's no solid place to land
in this present tense – the quiet lonely of a hole,
a park swing or buried deep in the clothing stack
at the back of a wardrobe
in a home thrown together
with fear and rough hands, drunk
and sideburned hair –
these cotton tributary dreams
so clean of language
you could dunk a thing
you could wash a rabbit

and from all this distance, see

the boy and the mother dancing –

one foot the next she is teaching him

to step all over himself

in time with her and again –

like hopscotch their legs,

like skipping rope their knees

bend and straightening up,

their bottoms knock and knock

a laugh so hard from their bellies –

now they are mashing potato

now hula-hooping

the mind recalls
blackcurrant juice bumped and sprawling
on the carpet
as the radio plays and the room is silent,
the hand of the boy up in shock or fright,
the mother – the first expletive he ever hears
out her mouth is an appeal to the universe
for his protection she runs
to gather a dishrag wet and dropping
to her knees plead-scrubbing her knuckles
to the floor till they almost bleed – O
the dreadful rapture of a car engine closing in

                      and from all this distance, rabbit
                      – see him, first off the block
                      when the deep voice hits again
                      worried little creature, spun away
                      when the man-shadow lifts
                      a thick limb, find him balled
                      behind a table leg or ducked
                      around a chest of Perspex drawers
                      emergency noise

in all the confined space

that one big bulb in the living room

spinning the corrugated man-hand

over everything

                              rabbit

suffering a whole place to ugly

like that – the house's fury

slamming its thorax everywhere outside

the wardrobe door again and down

the stairs, listen: it could be

tearing the room apart –

pissed in the hallway or

shouting a mother black, blue

from all this distance I am
whatever lessons there are to learn
and have to be forgotten:
a fading sofa, a carpet stain
emergency circling
its tinny blue lights across the teeth
perhaps what was needed
was to shake out the idea of a home
held in place by a hairpin
a shared desire to not
let the other play dead –

Alma, inside that wardrobe
take this uncooked speaking
from the belly of the boy
and throw it
to the bullying air –
tell him please again
if you squeeze your eyes tight
you are
arrived at a riverbed

> far away from
> a place of gone-
> bad eggs
> and hope-washed
> in water

A HISTORY

SHE

knew the kitchen she'd kept meticulous and
intimately knew the carpet she'd picked out years ago
and vacuumed every other day and the semi-comfy
two-piece the bedsheets that she even ironed and she
knew the TV with its local news that played about the
house – its walls so permanent and all the ornaments –
and she knew the man she tried to love
was in it all and all of it so rigidly in him
as all the money was, as was the car, her shoes
to some extent the boy in him and all her adult life
the world and how she saw it
and what was she to do – fixed
so definite within this state
– and where could any woman
who laid so resolutely in *the bed she'd made*
take her extant self and leave to

SHE

had to *lie in it* when resentment filled him up like whiskey each morning he would go out to the building site cold and masculine return bang on time with dinner steaming on the table and

SHE

had to *lie in it* when he didn't meet her gaze or smile no bit of boyishness beneath the surface when their child picked up his fork same time his father didn't notice instead his adult-breathing seemed to hold a swearword, he often skulked into another room clenched and sat building up his anger in front of the local news

SHE

sometimes has a place she wanders to
when it's all gone wrong barefoot on
the kitchen carpet – the uproar of his
voice at the doorframe or right hand's
swift speaking leaves her dumbstruck,
wringing out a dishcloth in her own
upright and desperate self, her im-
moveable body – she somehow
walks away from it and goes to find
the boy crawled underneath the sofa
or behind the wardrobe door inside
his room, she shrinks herself to sit
beside him there upon the softness of
the jumpers nicely smelling linen and
they each lean against the promise of
a song, a story that she used to tell,
the one about the magic river is his
favourite one

SHE

had to *lie in it* as the boy leapt across the room –
the pain inside the noise – his forehead met the sharp
edge of the wooden table to dodge a sudden ———
the swelling happened there in front of her
in real time the father's tantrum cooling and
she had to lie with her arm around him in the backseat
explaining to the boy the *accident*
and how the nurses might not understand he *tripped*
when they were *playing* – the full confusion
on his face, she saw some part of him fall away
some part of her dropped with it

★

there exists no document no evidence of any singular event nor photo of the inciting incident around which it all clicked into place – a piling up perhaps one thing stacked atop the next an adult lifetime's worth of shoulders groaning under unkind words, the husband's moods that changed the climate of the walls, bad language slammed against the cupboard doors and skid-marked pants and hoovering and hot and hurting cheeks and washing socks and scratchcards, the drying up his deadbeat eyes neither evidence nor any one inciting incident

but the boy

and perhaps a piling up of meanness cheap as cheap detergent brillo pads on the knuckles and that time the

husband kicked a cat and the ironing
board's broken frame and scrubbing
piss dried on the toilet seat and grease
and forearms burnt on chip fat no
singular incident

        but the boy

but perhaps the piled-up work-day
afternoons, she sat sometimes alone
in the carpet's swirling centre, the
world turning around her and how
she baulked at any sudden noise –
a spoon falling from the kitchen
countertop, the toaster springing up,
no singular event but one thing
stacked perhaps atop the next

        and the boy –

and what was she to do – fixed so permanently
to this state and where could
any woman take
her extant self

and child

and

leave

to

★

there exists no photo of the childhood bedroom its blinds pulled down to the windowsill no photo of the room its posters and its quarter-open drawers no photo could of course pick up the scent of rabbit on the unmade duvet, lamp switch, or his thumbprint on the wardrobe door towards which she again is somehow moving somehow slightly different this time more resilient something maybe taking hold although her body is still still and silent in the kitchen

A QUESTION

how much love does it take
to shrink a mother
away from her body
to the size of a little girl
with a smudge on her nose
how brave does that love have to be
tiptoeing through the fuming home
to find the boy tucked deep into his hiding
to climb in there beside him
and lift him in this filled-up moment
not this time by song or speaking
but out to journey
to coax him now to step
(gentle, rabbit) with her
into the footprints
of their favourite story
of water

and how much courage
can a boy-
rabbit receive –
see him untucking himself
careful-moving in that cramped space
between its jumbled contents – a pair
of his old baby shoes, some too-small
shirts, a robot toy or two, a box full
of forgotten pencil drawings long tidied away,
the music that his thinking makes
as it emerges, slowly, slowly,
from beneath the portents
of its worry – to take the hand
of the girl with freckles on her face

and what can the vocabulary
of the small girl's presence stir
in the tummy of the boy or spur,
this time, in his rabbit limbs
– see them cautious, one by one
grow unstuck from that which stuck them there

Alma, it's like her soft-speaking turns
the volume
out there down
– the wallpaper
shimmering muted towards its yellow
the shadow-dad shaking
quiet into his drink
the engine of his temper
almost mimes its cooling
like sleepy wild dogs

tired-eyeing a kitten
on the way to their slumber
and silent is the body of the mother
still left standing upright in the kitchen

and from all this distance the mind recalls
– eyes closed and forgetting for a minute
the pile of clothes, the cracked plastic
of the sock basket and bedsheets
neatly folded – that boy's cotton dreaming, with her
out and into the warm evening,
the sky with its streetlights coming on,
the tiled rooftops of the terraced homes
where other families settle down, feel
hope rise across the stretch of railway track
past the shops and up and wider, see, the length
and lushness of the muddy fields, the plush
wet and grassy riverbank is more vivid
and sudden-real

SHADOWGRAPHY

imagine the mind is a single wall and memory a single light shone directly onto its two-dimensional surface

    imagine the mind's walled surface and its singular beam of light constructs a type of ocular theatre in which all memory can be performed

    could be the whirring background noise is an old projector – its skittishness inferring perhaps the nervousness on the part of the narrator here, seeking, as he is, an alternative way to articulate the thing he needs to say

    imagine the theatre of the mind with its two-dimensional surface and its moon-like light, with the nervy projector in the background, are the conditions into which a story can be induced through use of silhouette

and know the use of silhouette – a vocabulary itself, in part, of absence, a blocking out, in part, of light – is a way this story doesn't have to look itself directly in the eye

when a thick black vertical line appears quavering on the left, there, of the two-dimensional surface, the wall, inside the theatre, let's say we recognise this line to be the outer edge of a wardrobe door, and from its lower part we see one tiny scrap emerge and then retract and when we see it slow-announce itself again we recognise that it's the foot of a creature, tentative, testing the temperature of the room

and we can read some potential risk here for the creature – some environmental danger he is troubling himself into

but when said foot touches what we know to be the floor, through the fact of the foot's sturdy placement, we can understand the creature to which this foot belongs understands in turn there is nothing in this immediate space to fear as yet and so we see a second foot or paw commit itself a little more to the act of stepping

★

the theatre of the mind – imagine a gesture – the sweeping of a palm across its single source of light – less than a second, blackness as transition – illuminates the creature in its full and shaky aspect

one virtue of the use of silhouette, its play on absence and its two-dimensionality afford a type of intuition to its audience, the value of which is that we might begin to read onto the blankness of the character an emotion, and so too the space through which he edges, or endow said blankness with a type of feeling, an interiority suggested by common experience – a sense of empathy

so here we confer innocence onto the profile of this creature, a vulnerability when the creature trembles slightly, falters for a moment – his flat shape flitting back-to-front – we appreciate his doubt, and join him in attempting to conjure the sureness of his movement

and when a second tiny figure then reveals its restive self from the outer edge of wardrobe door – when it appears, a cut-out with contours of a dress and hair in bunches, when it takes the creature's hand – it's like we ourselves have through our own good conscious wishes, hopefulness and magic thinking conjured her

and immediately we know her as the source from which the creature's brave and nurtured will-to-motion is assembled

and we are both animated
and relieved then as they do begin
slow, hand-in-hand and quiet-in-their-
clumsiness, to move from one side to
the other of what by now we might
conjecture is a bedroom

★

the theatre of the mind – imagine
through a gesture – the sweeping
of an artful palm across the single
source of light – darkness for a
moment then

those two silhouettes – a
vocabulary of disclosure and conceal-
ment, a way through which a story
doesn't have to tell itself too directly

also in this new arisen
scene a jagged pattern of right angle

jutting from right angle, brought into sharper focus, and we recognise it as a staircase

and we can read onto the rickety nature of this staircase an expression of the anxiousness the two figures hold inside their chests as they now work their hesitant way down and down its steps

★

a histrionic pause, a beat of nothing, in this context might be used to build expectancy or suggest a confluence of tension, an exaggerating darkness – a palm held over the lens, the single source of light – or might indicate a shift of tone or register a sense of dread – like pressing down the deepest note of an organ

a suspension of action in this context is an act of suspense, the building of a monument of knowing that the source of dread is waiting somewhere

so even when the palm is lifted, perhaps that note of dread remains and through the play of shadow, light, what we observe newly now is a room in which is housed a sleeping giant figure of a father – reclined in the cut-out shape of ugly armchair

his figure grows large, looming on the wall of the theatre of the mind then receding slightly then he's big again and so on – a rhythmic pattern which mimics a menace of deep breathing, snores, the sense that to waken him would be the end of everything

★

sleight-of-hand, a palm whipped once more away – then light – a trick of theatre reveals that room again, and we know through intuition now the two small characters have to travel through it, a room we also know contains the giant father – feel how the cavernous breathing of his slumber distorts their passage through this landscape, though we cannot at the moment see him

and then we do: sleeping cut-out figure in his armchair, in the far bottom corner of the picture, small then intensifying, slight then magnified across the whole of space, so we understand why they decide to pause a minute – catch their worry by the sleeve, the flatness of their bodies flashing left then right

when they continue on
their creeping-silent way across the
lit-up choppy sea of what has to be
the living room, they hardly appear
it seems to move at all

it seems that objects are
instead float-wobbling towards them
– giving the impression, through trick
of theatre, of their extenuating voyage:

the note of dread, here
comes the dad-sized pair of shoes
they have to jump over, and here's
a thick black frame of coffee table
under which they stoop,

and on this goes and on
this goes again – the arm end of a
sofa, an ashtray, a glass intractable
upon the floor – each object is nego-
tiated, punctuated by the shadow of

the father, perilous in his slumber, expanding to encroach upon the scene before fading back to the corner of the screen

and when they've finally made it through the jeopardy and tension of that room, and thank god they do, it's like the finger that's been holding down the note of dread is lifted and we open into the relief and brightness of the kitchen with its big rectangular door there, right there, their break for freedom –

O wonderful escape –

        but we know,

        somehow, back

        in the baseness

        of the living

        room the

        shadow of the

        sleeping father

has snapped itself
awake

THE MOTHER'S BEDTIME STORY
(A FRAGMENT)

it came to pass   a wrangling free
from the bad home's fist or an attempt to –
its language bawling even when it's not
its grip knuckling
the throat and loud even when it's sleeping

by language it is meant kindness rare as pocket change
and by language it is meant shame and dirty teeth

a shadow of a mad and angry man, his stirring,
drunk-woken and pots and clattering pans
and whiskey

the boy with his long ears or the girl
who is moving now a little faster with him
through the kitchen out the back door
towards a further place away –
the articulate love   of water

A HISTORY

WHEN SHE

    left her adult body this time she left
behind her adult body and the body
of the boy and took that other part
of him or maybe he took the part
of her that never had the chance to
grow and move the way it should
have, took it by the hand and though
there is no photo here they are:
running off hop-splashing through
the puddles

when she left her adult body she left her
adult body silent-staring out the window
of the kitchen

    and it was a strange thing and beautiful to have the boy's hand in hers and
without the weight she'd left behind
she felt something in her loosen
into joy

when she left her body she left
her body numb and heated near
the unforgiving oven

        the spark of childhood in the boy's
        palm she was holding – its lack of the
        old fear – wrote itself all over all her –
        she knew for a moment she could
        take a step and then the next step and
        the next

when she left her body she left her
adult body sitting on a kitchen stool
– the TV in the other room playing
loud and the shadow of a sleeping
man somewhere in there stirring,
coming to, rubbing at his eyes

A JOURNEY

PASSED THE WASHING LINE

one bedsheet in the sun on the patio, hung
very straight perfect-white – it's dreaming up
another sheet just the same they'd hang
almost identical still, the sheets
pegged inches apart
as if they are siblings
if this was a normal home
there would be siblings knotted and laughing –
if the sheets were siblings they would be happy
there are no children in the garden no friends
a patch has turned the one sheet darker
in the middle like a bad thought
all around the garden nothing else is happening,
a few bits of litter, sweet wrappers
stuck in the plant pot, leaves

which a while later
are left whirling

LEAVING THE ALLEY BEHIND

with its sad and rusted-looking
shopping trolley no child now can snugly fit
inside its seat –
as is the want of any small child
to know itself as safely held, to know
itself as densely packed, feet not touching
the mucky floor –

the trusted frame bent out
of purpose, divested of its wheels
the supermarket floor the trolley cannot again know
just as years ago it could not know its end was this:
to be left browning on its side, alone

in the
morbid shadow
of a livid left-behind dad slow-stalking
over the hard grey ground

INTO THE TOWN CENTRE

no windows on the graveyard stretch of concrete, no
windows yet in the promised flats, half-built
across a decade, and a tunnel:

follow that tunnel under the main road:
here come the windows of the shop, the blue-blue
café's windows plasticky and pasties and steaming
ugly soup then cherry Coke then muffins then
the windows of the bus station

                                          in their reflection
                              magnified and magnified again
                            you maybe if you strained enough
                                could see the rough bereft
                          and upset figure of the husband

JUICEBOX

    the uncobbled tarmac of the back road
    the feeling of the whole town gone
    bad – done, receding into the middle-distance
    far-flung faring, further away –
    the boy, smell of him untroubling
    towards the future

        Alma, the half-full juicebox excited and possible
                in the satchel
                and outside the satchel
            something wider, more definitely living:

                the boy, taking everything he had
                    he made it the shape
                    of everything he wanted
                closing his eyes and knowing
                      here you were

A HISTORY

SHE

left her body not looking over its shoulder, when it felt the absence of his gaze or unkind word her body closed its eyes while that other part of her that left stayed woken in another tense

                              there
                              were
                              trees
                              and
                              the
                              sky
                              over
                              them
                              was
                              safe
                              as
                              a
                              very
                              good
                              parent

beyond what's beyond
thought this moment
– it felt like it was al-
ways here along the
road and also hardly
felt like it was here
at all

        and moving tossed
        her heart ahead of her
        across a field remem-
        bering its way or
        growing into youth
        it felt like Christmas
        – fairy-lit – or felt like
        skipping school, and
        calling from the not-
        too-far-off distance:
        running water

★

there exists the possibility somewhere (there must) a photo of the plush and sloping grass that leads a wonky path towards the taller patchy reeds beyond which there's a river – you can (you must be able to) in this photograph catch sight of the still, moving slightly, cooling water and you can (it must be possible to) read into the frame somehow the figure of the boy running absolutely overwhelmed by love

absolutely overwhelmed by love
the mind smudging into
the blown-out present tense back here
when their little fingers touch touched are touching,
Alma when the lightness of your arm's hairs
your palm on his neck
his shoulder
the way you formed a perfect silhouette
marching over the marshy land and grass and

see him, rabbit up a tree, legs dangling from its thick
supportive branch, see him galloping excited,
running concentric circles in the mud

        you made it
        were
        making
        in this moment
        one nougatine victory

    see him almost ecstatic
towards the path towards the water

yodelling ahead

I AM THE RABBIT

the kindness in him welling

like he is carrying

a wrapped-up Easter egg

        and it matters –

        the chopped-up light

        language dropping out the present tense

        like sheet lightning

Alma, underscored by the touch that home has had

that home has had its own toxic grammar
that you both for a minute   didn't you
stepped outside

★

there exists somewhere (there must)
the possibility of a photograph taken
too close up to a young girl's smudged
nose flush to the half-moon of a boy's
face – the plumpness and affection
of this moment pinning them to the
reddening sky

THE MOTHER'S BEDTIME STORY
(A FRAGMENT)

when the boy with fluffy toes and big front teeth had crept with his little friend from underneath the hot-tempered home's roof and past the garden's washing line and snuck along the eerie alley and out across the town with its inculcating tunnels, his whiskers bristled with anticipation, as he set foot on a grassy stretch his hand alive inside the skinny fingers of his friend – they felt the light breeze guide them towards the sound of water off ahead with its gentle music almost enough to make them both forget the chorus of a shadow-dad – somewhere back there its murmuration, faint pans and whiskey glass, hurt and eyes as wide as acorns

SHADOWGRAPHY

a palm receding from a lens, a cylinder of light alighting on a wall, the trick of two dimensions inducing the conditions in which a story can continue being spoken of a creature running flatly – hand-in-hand – with his friend, a plucky girl with bunches in her hair

we know this use of silhouette as a lexicon of absence – in part a blocking out, in part a way a story or its teller doesn't have to look all of its disquiet directly in the eye

here are the two dark cut-outs in an open field, we recognise it by the outlines of its hedgerows which are travelled right to left across the bright-lit two dimensions of the wall to effect upon the viewer the sense of the movement of the scene

and the way in which they totter, the creature and his friend, makes it evident that said tottering is resultant of a knowing in this moment a cautious type of joy

★

the connective tissue of remembering is built when sensor modals of the brain read individual gestures of a given object or a situation, and these individual gestures are kept in extant and concomitant tension with other readings of said object's or said situation's gestures, joining each to each then suggests the whole

so we might know, say, a
shoe through our visual system by
the gesture of its shape, and/or know
it by the gesture of its dour odour,
through our olfactory system, and
we might know a shoe through our
auditory system by the gesture of
its getting louder as it slaps against
the floor, or know the father's shoe
through the gustatory system by the
specific fear that loiters in the mouth

the connective tissue of
remembering arises when a gesture
of one object or a situation becomes
a gesture to them all

★

the field – we might watch the
gesture of two cut-outs playful on
this backdrop, one might perform a

spontaneous leap of joy, one might do a cartwheel in expression of its sudden-felt and momentary freedom, but these single gestures to that freedom can't help also signifying what this momentary experience of being free is experienced as freedom *from*

when we see these cut-outs clumsy-balancing their way in turn along the elongated shape of fallen tree trunk, the gesture of this act collapses the distance between this present tense and all the fearful rooms through which they previously careful-trod to get here

and as one cut-out stoops to smell a flower and the flower sudden-magnifies to demonstrate to us, the viewer, its importance in this beatific second, we might read into its amplification, through trick of light and two dimensions, the gesture of the ogre-father's breathing – his own magnification as he slept, the threat he posed of waking, and recall the fact he did indeed awaken and that he is growing larger somewhere just outside the scene

A HISTORY

SHE

felt the tug of adulthood's common-
sense distinct and real
as a distant husband's
fingers tightened on her waist

        SHE

        felt the tug of possibility in
        the boy's touch wrapping
        round her wrist –

                SHE

        felt the tug of possibility –
                the river
            the firm grip of the
                husband
          the child, the child

A QUESTION

for how long can a small boy run outside his home's corporeal parts beneath a new and beatified sky saying look, look at this – evergreens, and the dazzle of birds in flight towards the water you can step in – simple as wanting, not simple enough, too simple – with the relentlessness of carpet back there and ashtrays, and chubby peanuts left uncracked in the cupboard – for how long can he run outside the image of a father sozzled in the armchair – all five fingers down his own snoozing trousers – for how long can a child waken in the possible-something-more – the opened-up present you can almost simply walk into and the mind recalls they were – weren't they – making all this happen-possible love right here and no bad work no cheap blaspheme or hungry swearword up ahead rejoicing and no scratchcard or spilled chip fat – the stillness there, the noiseless wind and faint birdsong, the moment alight and huge and please let them enter in, taking off their shoes

                                          Alma
                                          they
                                          had
                                        hadn't
                                          they
                                            at
                                        this
                                    moment
                                       near-
                                   escaped

and look, the boy, Alma, up ahead – no bruise
no torn shirt by the river no childhood's mean tongue
no stung lips by the river no cat kicked – all the TV
remotes of the world are in their place in the opened-
up present   it's like they can walk out on this water
– see, he's taking off his shoes as a palm sweeps
across the lens –

[let me stick my cotton fingers in my ears]

does the body keep the home or does the home keep the body

THE MOTHER'S BEDTIME STORY
(A FRAGMENT)

in the meadow-like grassy patch, rabbit-lungs how they flap and breathe and laugh mid-air and the song of leg and muscle and cheek by tooth the rabbit runs upright see him almost dance excited in his ankle bones the boy in cotton trousers and beside him her presence real and only one of them is taking notice of the turgid shadow-dad and ornaments rumbling, snapped teeth carried in a bag and thunder-clatter that's closing in, closing in

A HISTORY

SHE

felt intuitively
this might be
too good to
be real, truly
the night
fresh on their
faces like a
time before
she knew
the world
in all its
immolating
cruelty

her body wore the oven gloves and
pulled the dishes out the heat of the
open oven door and her body wiped
the surfaces hoovered up the floor

                              this dragging

                                      sense

                              in the cortex

                                 something

                            silent-waiting

                              like the sting

                          from a parent's

                              hand after

                        skipping school

                        or a husband's

                            breathing on

                                the neck

inevitable
like a day-trip
going rotten
in touching
distance of
its destination
when just
before you
are forced
to turn back
you can
for a second
glimpse it –

ARTICULATE RIVER

O Alma, a hymn to all that is possible – that river soaking clean everything that ever went bad a wet hymn to the flat-roofed pub and the men in brilliant tracksuits wet the husband on the way home and the arm of the wife still and absolutely drenched the cheek of the sad mum and the boy's buck teeth drenched the hand back in the kitchen here we are a hymn to the yellow light hymn to the wrung stomach and tender skin

        and Alma, look ahead, up there a thousand other rabbits and their own tiny smudged-nosed friends bobbing there floating like illuminated lanterns

        the river complete around them in its absorbing love a language washing the undone present – only brilliant water as a palm sweeps across the lens –

SNOW

they imagined didn't
they, Alma, they got
forgiven for leaving
were allowed to go
everything they'd
ever known holding
their wrists and feet
sleeves and backsides
so many hands
on the body thrown
up and celebrated –
like birthday bumps –
lips light on the
ceiling then caught
and again –
their stomachs
through the air
his chemoreceptor
is butterscotch
in the blood

so much love

is stuffed

with vanilla

salt her inner-ear

corn syrup

my own throat filling with alkaline

and treacle from all this distance

thank you

I am soft-cracked

and laughing

myself hoarse

                happy as happy

as a snowman

melting

as the lens darkens –

one hand

one pan

one pot

one shoe

a chorus

rabbit

sudden-alone

a palm swept

over a projector lens

Alma, where did you go

see him, the boy

sat down

in its straight-lit promenade, the river

its tight-knit vernacular, the river

his trouser legs

tucked into a pair

of socks,

the quiet yellow-lit

nothing new

can get in at him now

here, like a wardrobe

the world outside, look

its grey love gone, going

inside his quiet song:

king of nervous laughter
like a shop window breaking
into shopping bags
or a bad sculpture hugging its kneecaps
and beneath a red swing
till dinner goes cold in the pedal bin
if you prayed to your mum's
one good dress
like ants in a biscuit tin
for the kitchen light's off-switch up
so you can drip into bed
if hope or its passing
flooded your mouth
and your tongue is dead then
you know my name

see him,

tiny sacred thing shaken

in its collarbones

his mind in the mud –

or buried beneath a bridge

alone along the river

while the wind is being gathered

there is so much wet here and moving

it aches

his shut eyes

to know about   help, tell me:

Alma, for a moment, where did you go

A QUESTION

for how long can a mother shrink her self and leave –
for how long can she last a step outside the body
outside the home and all its corporeal parts –
the carpet which she understands her own feet upon,
the walls to which her living has been fixed, all
the cupboards she has filled with her particular type
of care, the plinky whistle the hot tap makes when
it's twisted slowly clockwise – for how long can she
strain against the gravity of this place: its shadow
at the drunken table, how long – with its knuckles round
a housing deed, its fingers on a bank account –
can her girlish hopeful self run until she hits the edge
adulthood again and what she finds there slows her
down, makes her pause, take a sensible breath,
returns her to the stark and grown-up practicality
of home

A HISTORY

SHE

inside her body sat in front
of a TV's blare
and in the rigidity of her chair
knew only in a distant way
the joy of freedom,
glanced at
through a childhood's shining,
his eyes now, the husband's,
back and fixed
upon the back
of her body's permed
and greying hair

SHE

in her body sensed the fierceness in
his voice sometimes as very far away
an echo almost which contained a
version of the past that could not
reach her, then her body sensed the
fierceness in his voice sometimes as
very close, its heavy menace almost
hot as iron steam upon her face

SHE—

REVERSE

your voice Alma pulling me back off
the water and my voice over mudbanks
up the hill like a coach in reverse – Alma
over barbed wire your voice, mine
dragged by the ankles miles of asphalt
roof and chip fat your voice calling
mine through tin cans and cardboard
boxes brambles and Ribena stinging
nettles and dogshit your voice dragging
me back park and sandpit scratchcards
a hymn yellow-lit beneath a bridge
and pedal bin dog-bite your call
beckoning mine as laughing pulling
me backwards your voice pub-like
and maternal freckles densely packed
children's hairpins and nylon washing
line pots and plates thumbprint on a
wardrobe door you know my name
back inside it and embossed upon
wallpaper the mind the mind

CONNECTIVE TISSUE

the theatre, the two-dimensional wall, a light shone by an old projector, a narrator who doesn't want to look his story too directly in the eye

    the lit-up white space of that wall and the whole potential of its landscape, what fearful adventure lay there for the two characters who negotiated its terrain – the tiny figures through the trepid home, the fleeing and the wobble and wonder of the open field, its pathway to a hope-filled river and their pocketing of fistfuls, for a moment, of love

    onto their flat and moving silhouettes the reading of our own intensity of feeling – the wrested empathy and insight into what the figures have seen and known and stepped through

see: the wall, its light

what might the absence of these cut-out figures on its surface gesture towards now – the thick black line of wardrobe door alone in the theatre of the mind, this lit space bereft of rabbit and of little girl – the narrator: what it is that he cannot say – listen: the whirring old projector

ACKNOWLEDGEMENTS

Thank you to all of my friends, family and peers who have in immeasurable ways made this book happen, particularly Joey, Susie, Mark, Emily, Lucy, Kaveh, Max, Paige, Anthony, Alex, Jack, Amy, Ray, Kristina, Sarah, Rachael, Kieran, Martha, Marsha, Robin at Makina, and the folks at The Poetry Society. Heartfelt gratitude to Imogen and Claudia from Greene & Heaton, and to Joanna and the team at Simon & Schuster. I'd like to acknowledge Clarice Lispector, whose influence echoes at moments in this book. I'd like to highlight Joseph Pintauro, whose singular work I have carried, often physically, with me for over twenty years, and Greg Therriault, the manager of Joseph's estate, for his support and encouragement. Lastly, thank you to Rebecca and Finn, for the innumerable ways you make my life habitable and fun.

This book takes its title and point of departure from Joseph Pintauro's *The Rabbit Box* (1970), the Spring Volume in the seasonal quartet that makes *The Rainbow Box*.